Walt Disney's
DUMBO and the Circus Train

On the track near the Big Top
stood the circus train.

The circus was almost ready
to move on.

When the animals finished their acts,
they boarded the train.

The lions, seals, bears, and tigers were
ready to go. And o topus too.

The elephants were hard at work helping
the circus men.

They had already taken down some of
the tents.

There was still plenty to do.
But one elephant was not helping.
He was still in the Big Top.

That elephant was Dumbo the Flying
Elephant, star of the circus.
He and his friend Timothy Mouse
were still flying in the Big Top.
The people kept clapping.
They did not want to let Dumbo go.

"Dumbo never helps. He has an easy life," said one of the working elephants as she lifted a heavy load.

"It's not fair. I wish we could get rid of him," said another elephant.

"I have an idea," said the first elephant. "Come with me."

The two elephants went over to
Dumbo's private car.

It was at the very end of the train.

The elephants waited till no one
was looking.

Then one of the elephants quickly
loosened the hook that held Dumbo's car
to the next one.

At last the show in the Big Top was over.
Dumbo and Timothy walked out of the tent.
Then Dumbo gave Timothy a ride over to
the train.

Acting in the Big Top was hard work.
Dumbo and Timothy felt very tired.

They went right into Dumbo's car.
They never saw the loose hook.

Dumbo and Timothy went straight
to bed.

In no time they were fast asleep.

While they slept, the Big Top was
loaded onto the circus train.

Now the train was ready to leave.

Through the night the train traveled.
It chugged across peaceful fields.
When the engineer drove through
a sleeping town, he tooted softly.

Late in the night the train started
to climb up a long, steep hill.

Little by little the loose hook on
Dumbo's car gave way.

Before the train reached the top
of the hill, the hook opened!

Dumbo and
Timothy woke up.
Something
was wrong!
They looked
out the window.
"Oh, my!" said
Timothy. "Oh, my!
We are going
the wrong way!"

Dumbo's car was rolling backward!
Faster and faster it sped down the track.

"Help!" yelled Timothy.
But nobody heard.

A trainman heard Dumbo's car coming.
Another train was on the same track.
There was going to be a crash!
Just in time the trainman pulled a switch.

Dumbo's car turned safely
onto another track.
At last it came to a stop
in a quiet meadow.

At dawn Dumbo and Timothy
climbed out of the car.

They wanted to know where they were.
Some crows were sitting in a tree.
"Have you seen the circus train?"
Timothy asked the crows.

"The circus train?" said a crow.
"It went by on the main track
a long time ago."

"We MUST find the train!"
said Timothy. "Dumbo is
the star of the circus.
He has a show to do tonight."

"The train must be far away by now," said Timothy to Dumbo. "But you can fly us to it."

The crows showed Timothy and Dumbo
the way to the main track.
"Thank you for your help," said Timothy.
And he and Dumbo flew off.

Dumbo and Timothy flew and flew.
At last they found the circus train.
It had stopped at a river.
A big flood had washed away the bridge.

The ringmaster was very upset.

Dumbo was missing.

And the train was stuck.

"What are we going to do" he said. "We have a show tonight."

Just then Dumbo and Timothy flew down.
The ringmaster was very happy to see them.
Suddenly he had a bright idea.
"I think I know how we can fix the bridge,"
the ringmaster said. "We're lucky that
Dumbo can fly."

Soon Dumbo and Timothy were
in the air again.

They were carrying a letter from
the ringmaster to the next town.

Dumbo flew straight to
the town's railway station.
He found the repair shed.

Dumbo gave the letter to
the railway man.

The railway man read
the letter.
In it was a list of
the things needed
to fix the bridge.

AT YOUR SERVICE

NUTS
BOLTS
NAILS
LUMBER
ROPE
TOOLS

Back at the train the ringmaster said,
"We're going to need everyone's help."

The ringmaster opened the cages
and let all the animals out.

Before long Dumbo came
flying back to the train.

He was carrying a big sack
of tools and parts.

The animals were all
waiting for him.

Now they could begin
to fix the bridge.

The elephants, monkeys, giraffes, leopards, and even the ostriches helped.

Dumbo flew back to the station for more parts.

He brought everything that the animals needed.

Everybody helped.
The elephants carried the lumber.
And the monkeys built a crane.

Bit by bit the bridge was fixed.
Soon there was only one thing
left to do.

The monkeys tied a rope to
the broken track and...

"One, two, three, hup!" the ringmaster called.
Everyone pulled together on the rope.
The broken track was lifted into place!
Now the train could cross the bridge.
The circus show could go on!

Soon the circus train was at the station.
The whole town was there to greet it.

That night Dumbo gave a fine show.
But he felt very tired.

When the show
was over, Dumbo
went right to
his car.
He just wanted
to sleep.

But what was this?

In front of his car were all
the circus folk.

"Hurrah for Dumbo!" they cried.
"He saved the show!"

"I take back what I said before,"
said a big elephant. "Dumbo
does help us. He helps
in his own way.
We couldn't do
without him."

And everyone
cheered.